MONSTRA MODERNA

WEREWOLF

"Where the fuck is she?"

The slap ripped me back into consciousness, my ears ringing under the tectonic blow.

"Huh?"

The blurry figure gripped me by my shirt, actually lifted me off the seat, and slapped me with such force that I fell to the ground with a groan. I spit out the salty blood that had begun pooling in my mouth.

Fluorescent lights flickered above my heard swirling around like leaves on a pond.

"Do not…fucking…PLAY WITH ME!"

The steel toe boot crashed against my ribs, the bursting pain exploding in my side.

I coughed, my own blood splattering upwards like a fountain and splashing down on my face.

"Wait…" I wheezed. "Please…"

Two more debilitating blows caught me on the right side, the crunching and cracking of my ribs sounding like Rice Krispies.

Then I was up again, staring into the desperate blue eyes of my assailant. He was crying.

"Please. Where is my daughter?"

He thrust me backwards into the chair and almost knocking it completely over.

"Why are you doing this?" He asked.

"Sir, I…please let me go… I have no idea…what you're talking about…please." I wheezed, my lungs pressure on my splintered ribs felt like hot hellfire.

"QUIT WITH THE FUCKING BULLSHIT. I KNOW IT WAS

YOU."

This time, it was a closed fist punch that rocked my cheek. His metallic rings collided with my jaw sending two of my molars flying against the wall and clattering harmlessly to the floor.

He gripped my greasy hair, and whipped my neck back so hard I thought it would break. I stared into his pleading eyes, bloodshot with either rage or exhaustion.

Suddenly, he reached into his belt. I figured he caught on to the fact that I really knew nothing and was about to put nine millimeters of lead into my skull, but he just pulled out an iPhone and thrust it into my hand.

A video was playing. I watched staticky doorbell camera footage through the tint of my own blood and tears. The scene depicted a narrow portion of the front yard, and the road strip beneath a dim streetlight along the front of it. Then, from the right side of the frame, a man trotted gaily, holding the hand of a little girl down the sidewalk.

The man was me.

"Sir please, I...I was never there... I just woke up here..." I sputtered out.

A blow to the gut forced a coughing spray of blood from my lungs.

Then there was a desert eagle pointed at my forehead.

"I WILL BLOW YOUR FUCKING BRAINS OUT IF YOU DON'T TELL ME WHERE THE FUCK MY DAUGHTER IS."

"I, ok." I stammered. "Please just let me up."

The man hoisted me to my feet so I stared at his eyes, full of dry tears.

"We are going to get back in my truck, and you are going to take me to my daughter. One chance, if you even fucking *ponder* taking me to anywhere other than my daughter's location, I'll have a hell of a goddamn time cleaning your brains off my dash. Before that though, we'll go straight to your baby mamas place, and I'll blast your son's skull off, and make you hold him in your arms."

"You sick fuck." I spat a spray of blood and venom at him.

"Don't you play the morality card with me you fucking

hypocrite!" He swung a right hook, shattering my orbital into pieces with the metallic butt of his pistol.

Rain glazed the car windows, the fog of my mind dense and oppressive. The barrel of the weapon was pointed at the base of my skull. I could feel it poking the back of the neck every time I hit a pothole. One flick of this crazy fucks finger and I was swimming with the fishes. But it was starting to dawn on me that maybe I was the one who was losing it. There was no doubt about it... it was me in the video.

It wasn't me. It couldn't be. A doppelganger? A set-up somehow? Either way, it was definitely me with oblivion three inches from my grey matter, so I had to do something.

I had no idea where I was going. Not a clue. He told me to drive so I did. But I didn't have this guy's fucking daughter. I had to make a plan.

The police station was out, I could already imagine the bullet penetrating my cranium the second he saw me pull into the driveway. I could smell the crazy on the fucker mixed with overpowering, rotten egg BO. I could crash the left side of my car into a cement pole, jump out and run for it. And either break my spine or get shot in the back as I made my daring escape. It wouldn't fly. I could get my gun. A Mossberg 590A1, enough firepower to blast the fucker back to wherever he came from. But it was locked away in my gun safe, in my room, in my apartment.

But it was the only damn chance I could think of. Plus, pulling into my dilapidated buildings parking lot would give the sicko reassurance, it would be the exact kind of lowkey place where someone would hide a body. If someone needed to hide a body, which of course I didn't.

"Where are we going?" He asked, pleaded. "You better be fucking taking me to her, and so help me God if you hurt one hair on her scalp I will personally filet you with a butterknife. Are you taking me to her?

"...yes." What the fuck else could I say?

The car bumped along the backroads of the city to it's outskirts. The twelve-story apartment seems to exist for no reason at all, constructed in the middle of a field with no neighbours and left to rot, to be forgotten. Originally it was supposed to be used for cheap housing, but even the poorest people didn't wanna live there. Except for the lowest of the low that is.

"This the place?"

"Ya."

"Then go."

The musty yellow lobby was empty, and the buzzer system hadn't worked in years. We just slipped through the screen door, the buildings systems unable to stop any intruder that wanted in.

Then we were in my apartment. The coffee table was crowded with hollow, brown glass bottles. The 90s style box TV, left on, illuminated the dark space with the dancing white light of static. Two woven lawn chairs, one pink, one black were the only other pieces of furniture in the conjoined living room kitchen.

To the immediate right, due to poor planning, was the bathroom door. Across the main space, the only other door led to my tiny bedroom. Where I kept my shotgun.

"Where is my daughter?" He growled, drilling the barrel of his Desert Eagle into the spot my spine joined my skull.

"She's… she's in there, in the bathroom." I said, gesturing to the door to the right.

That's where he fucked up. He opened the door himself, and with a quick swivel I shoved him and slammed the door. I heard him crash to the floor, and booked it across the room knocking over my pink lawn chair.

I slammed my bedroom door behind me and set to work on the safe. I fumbled with the keys in what felt like slow motion, like I was dreaming. In fact, the whole thing felt like a dream. It wasn't real, it couldn't be.

My Mossberg was hot in my hand. Blood, both dark brown and crimson red clung to the off-white tiled bathroom. Two corpses lay in the bathtub, one old, one young.

My chest was warm, and the world was still in a hazy fog that permeated all my dreams. But something was off, something was...hurting?

I looked at my shoulder, where a golf ball sized hole of meat, muscle and bone gaped. I put my finger in it and felt my shoulder blade. Now I'm here.

"So, you are suggesting that you don't remember murdering Rebecca and Jeremy Steele?"

"I'm suggesting I didn't kill anyone! That son of a bitch killed his daughter, tried to off me, then killed himself!"

"Why were they in your apartment?"

"What?"

"Why would Jeremy Steele take his daughter to your apartment, especially as you mentioned that you had not met Jeremy before, kill her there, fail to kill you, and kill himself there? If, as you suggest, Jeremy intended to kill his daughter, why would he go to a strangers house? You're story, Jack, is not adding up in the slightest."

"I..."

"I think that's all I need Jack. Thank you for your cooperation. And, may I just add, I wish the death penalty was still legal."

"Detective?"

"Hm?"

"Am I dreaming?"

WENDIGO

June 9, 2079

Today we leave. Mixed feelings. Excited about the pilgrimage, not excited about the ride. Keeping this e-journal is mandated by our sponsors, so I guess I'm just gointa write down my feelings and stuff.

The sis has been giving me spiders, if she's this bored on day one she's gointa be in for a long trip. I might just conk her out.

Dads been on lockdown. Quiet as a clam. Just sitting there reading his ancient essays. Real yawn stuff like Johnathon Swift.

I'm gonna keep busy in the VR room, it came decked with all the games. Cya next week I guess.

June 16 2079

A guy can only stimulate so much VR. I can't believe it's only been a week, feels like the last ten minutes of school on rerepeat. Hell, I even played real life cards with the sis.

Dad still just spends his time in the elibrary and talking science with ground control. Whole lotta bla bla bla.

He sounded more angry than usual, good thing I mastered the art of ignoring him back home. These close quarters are gointa make it harder though.

One week down, 16 to go.

I'm gointa noose it.

June 23 2079

We should finally hit the wormhole tomorrow, did I say finally?

Outside the viewers was nothing but twinkling stars lifetimes away. We couldn't even see the famous blue marble because it was so far behind us.

I'm goina little cabin crazy so I bet dad and Saila feel it too. Actually I know dads feeling it, he's no good at the whole feelings thing.

He yelled at Saila yesterday for spilling some milk. Literally I swore he was gointa cry with fury. I even saw him clench his fist, he ain't do that since I was 12. I was cocked and ready just in case I had to deck him. As spidery as the sis is he ain't gointa pick on her like he did me.

June 30 2079

How can I describe a colour you've never seen? From what I have heard, the wormhole feels something like a mushroom trip mixed with peyote and golba. Undulating ebbs and flows like an ocean, then suddenly explosions of greenish silverish purplish fireworks. That's the best I got. It almost made the snore fest flight worth it.

The sis was taped to the window, hypnotized by the display. I gotta say if she weren't such a twerp, she'd be kinda cute.

Dad had a meltdown today. Same way he did before mom left all pissed off, screaming huffing and puffing, slamming random appliances. Like a rampaging toddler with too much muscle. I know better than to ask him why when he's like that. I just took the sis into the VR room and tried to distract her, but even over the Hawaiian beach relaxation game we could hear the temper tantrum raging across the hallway. Saila wasn't frothing over or anything but I could tell by the way she scrunched her eyebrows that it was getting to her. A feeling I remembered all to well.

Hopelessness.

July 7, 2079

His rage ended with a fizzle after 6 days. He slumped in the captain's red swivel chair and cast his eyes downwards like the rage had physically worn him out.

Not complaining. But now the mood isn't so aggressive, it's just oppressive. His mood is so thick you can feel it in the air pressure. The sis has been slouching around, soaking up his energy. I'm pretty good at ignoring him but I miss Saila's normal annoying ass keeping me busy in this dull ship.

If he holds up I'm going to confront him. I'm not the same little kid anymore, I can speak up for myself.

July 14, 2079

Fucking Android prick. I don't know why I thought anything would change. Nothing ever does with him.

I asked him what his goddamn problem was and he told me it was me, like I've been the one yelling and screaming followed by a silent treatment. More and more I see him for the kid he really is. I thought that was gointa be all, but the prick gave me half a meal today! Like, are you kidding me? I woulda got some grub myself but he's locked the pantry by changing the password.

Saila tried to sneak me some of her dinner but I was all smoke and fumes and couldn't eat. I glared lasers at him. He met my eye, mundane fire blazing behind his pupils.

That was last night. Tonight was a light dinner too, just tomato soup and grilled cheese. The spaceship cheese tasted funny, probably from dehydration. I'm hungry as horse. Dad didn't say anything either. He ate in the main quarters while me and Saila ate in the dining room like normal.

I hate this piece of shit. Causes problems and is too pussy to even own up to it. Soon as we land I'm getting a job and getting the hell out.

July 21, 2079

I confronted dad about this dogfood bullshit. The final straw was when he served us literally bread, butter, and rice one day. He was pissed at first, huffing and puffing about me not knowing anything and being a selfish prick.

But then something in him broke. I've never seen anything like it before, his eyes glazed over and he collapsed into a chair.

"We don't have enough food." He began to weep.

I was uncomfortable, never seen the oaf cry before. I wrapped an awkward arm around his shoulders and pulled him in, told him it would be ok. He snorted out a muffled laugh through his snot and tears, and I thought he was going crazy. Turns out he was just laughing at how insane the idea of "being ok" really is.

The pantries lock clicked as he slid his card key over the cool blue panel. The gut punch hit harder than the hunger. There was....is.... nothing. It's like the second Great Depression. A few soup packets remained, a shaker of salt and two cans of peaches. Dad was allergic to peaches.

I sat down on the flat, metallic floor, my grey matter jumping at ways we could make it more than 10 weeks on scraps. There was nothing to eat in the void of space. Our own waste? The leather seats? The world was spinning.

Then I felt my dads big arm around me for the first time in eons.

"Don't worry son, we will get through this."

His resolve was almost enough to pull me out of it.

We could see Mars today due to some weird orbit thing I don't understand. It felt so much nearer, even if it was just a trick of the eye. Didn't matter anyway. Out course was charted. So close to Mars, yet so far from Venus.

August 28 2079

Even though I've been giving half my rations to the sis, she stills withering. It's almost more painful than the decaying pit that was my stomach. I've lost weight already and I can see my finger bones sticking out like vacuum sealed meat sticks.

None of us do much of anything these days. Just trying to conserve energy, but we all know, probably even Saila now, that none of this will make it out of this. It's over, probably due to some stupid oversight by the preparation team.

I'm too tired to write more. This will probably be my last log. It's been a pretty shit life.

August 3, 2079

We're officially out of food. Saila lays on the couch now nothing but a hollow husk. Dad has crusted over, locked himself up in the brain. I tried to talk to him once, ask him his plan, but he just ignored me completely as if I was a ghost in the wind. Maybe I am. I guess I was still holding on to the kid-style hope that somehow remained in me. Now it's really over.

Someone...someone's knocking on the doors.

It was... oh god... I just gotta...

August 4th 2079

I got to write it down. Not for the fucking company but for myself, I wish we had some old school pads and paper.

It was my dad who knocked on my door. He was dripping in blood, his eyes vacant as the space crawling past the windows at tantalizing pace. I thought he was hurt.

In his hands was a plate of fresh meat, cooked. He asked if I was hungry.

I said yes.

But deep in the pit that was my stomach, I knew what it was.

He told me to eat.

I asked him where the sis was.

He chuckled. Fucking chuckled. He took a sec to compose and reminded me that he always kept his promises.

I was hot with fury, but energy less. I pulled myself up out of the chair, and pushed past him towards the den.

There she was splayed out on the coffee table, gutted, and filleted like roadkill. Her face was tilted up reflecting the fading white light of the closest star. She wasn't scared, or shocked even. On her face was just…confusion. Like she couldn't figure out what was happening.

I would have cried, but I was too empty, too hollow.

I felt his hand on my shoulder. Like I did after I scored two touchdowns in my junior year. After I got an A. Like I seen him do to Saila after…what he did to Saila

My bony fist cracked across his nose shattering it and sending blood spewing. His hands flew up to defend himself, but I kicked his shin. While he was distracted with two sources of pain, I pulled his head down with the left and gave him three quick jabs to his stomach. He slumped.

The next thing I remember was looking at Saila's lifeless visage, and I don't think her face will ever leave me. I can't describe the fury that came over me. I stomped on his skull until it was a red a white stew that stuck to my boots. I have an extra pair though, thank god for fucking that. Extra boots, but no food. Except, well.

I can't let the meat go to waste, right? I can't just die when there is so much food. I would be crazy not to eat it...right?

August 10th 2079

I gotta write or else I might lose it. Have to.

I covered Saila with a blanket. No way I would eat her. But dad, on the other hand...well that son of a bitch would have done it to me. But how could I butcher my dear old dad?

Well, it turns out carving up your parents isn't so hard when you're a blink away from starvation. I could have just bit into his fat arms right there. But I still had enough in me to know to cook it though. Probably riddled with parasites.

So I took the biggest butcher knife we had. It was clean, unused, sharp. The problem was I had almost no strength left besides my own desperation to survive. Like a cornered animal.

I read once in school that bears will eat their own cubs to survive a hard winter. It's been rising for decades because of shrinking habitats and food sources. I asked my teacher how they could do that, eat their own kids. For them, she said, it's just about survival, not love. If the mother dies, the defenceless cubs will soon die too. If the mother makes it through the winter, she can always have more cubs. Her words rang in my head then, her telling me that animals are different than humans. It made sense at the time.

Now I get it. Love is just what we hide behind, to tell ourselves we are doing more than just surviving.

But love is nothing in the face of death.

The knife bit through my father's skin and into his fleshy thigh. It felt like... a thick orange, as the skin sliced away revealing the sweet, savoury flesh below. I plunged my knife into the meat and pulled back a stringy strip. I wanted to cook it, but I just couldn't wait. I held it above my head and slurped it up like...like spaghetti.

I'll go to hell if it wasn't the best thing I've ever tasted.

August 25th 2079

There isn't much meat on them left. We are all just skins and skeletons.

END OF LOG

The following excerpt was recovered from experimental ship journey designation 2138. "Starvation" level set to ten; standard results. Summary follows:

Subject's One and Three picked clean, just bones, hair and teeth remaining.

Subject Two survivability: 98.7%

Description: Subject Two was founded in his quarters with torn morsels of flesh piled high in the corner. Subject unaggressive until food stockpile approached.

Subject was subdued and placed in holding pen 11.

Status: Successful. Subject Two suggested for Venus protocol.

SÉANCE

The candles flickered, casting dancing shadows of orange and purple throughout the blackened room. Her work was precise, the crimson paint forming a perfect pentagram upon the floor. She lay in the center prostrate; her forehead pressed down on the ancient oaken hardwood so hard that she could feel the individual slivers. Blue moonlight seeped in through the thin slits of drawn curtains.

She began her chant, a croaky guttural Latin that seemed to emanate from somewhere else besides her mouth, somewhere deeper.

The candles flicked toward the door.

Downstairs, the front door slammed shut, a mini earthquake shaking the floorboards. Her heart slowed, and a paralysis crept into her tense and bruised muscles. Only her eyes moved, like little flies caught in jars. Something was coming up the stairs.

The farmhouse was over 100 years old, her grandmother had told her. Each ancient step croaked and groaned with it's own unique personality as a heavy mass lumbered upwards and closer, closer.

Something was coming. The atmosphere weighed down upon her, the breath escaped her lungs.

Wind howled and rattled the shingles, shook the forest that surrounded the house into a fray. A cool rain pattered a rhythm as inky clouds blotted out the blue moonlight. The last stair moaned it's final warning; it, *he*, was down the hall. The same hall where she had played marbles with her grandma.

She hadn't her marbles anymore.

The door rattled twice, as if a hulking mass was slamming it's weight against it. Forehead to hardwood, she dare not move from her prostrate position. The brass doorknob twisted the door groaned inward.

It's shadow encompassed her.

She felt a long fingernail loop around her waistband and viciously pull it downward, slicing the skin open. Then the lashes began.

It must have been a whip of fire for it seared so. She yelped in pain crying like an injured animal.

It wasn't supposed to be this way.

She dare not turn around, for she knew what was behind her was way worse than a demon.

If only the ritual had worked.

HAUNTINGS

"Breakfast!" Jonah called, his cheer echoing through the house. Maple bacon, pancakes, and coffee wafted the warm smell of nostalgia into the air. A good ol' Donner family traditional Sunday breakfast was the best way to start his day, as far as Jonah was concerned.

Sara plodded into the kitchen yawning. Her plaid pajamas and oversized white t-shirt threatened to swallow her whole as she rubbed her eyes.

"Morning Sunshine!"

"Mornin' dad." She plopped down at the table, staring dreamily into its shiny surface with glazed eyes.

Jonah crooked a smile; his daughter had always been hazy in the mornings, ever since she was just a tyke. On a plate, he piled a stack of pancakes with a warm slab of butter melting atop, and a cavity-causing amount of maple syrup. On the side, bacon, extra-crisp, just as she liked it. He filled her glass to the brim with golden orange juice.

May emerged from the bedroom with Cole's pudgy body resting upon her hip. Her flowy nightgown waltzed in the breeze, her beautiful skin glowing olive in the morning sun's rays that breached through the window. Her figure was gorgeous, astonishing as the first time he had seen it, Jonah nearly dropped the spatula.

Jonah slid his oven-mitted palm behind her waist and pulled her in for a passionate kiss. He transferred Cole into his free arm and May pulled away. He studied her oaken eyes, the colours of the forest dancing in the sunlight.

"God am I lucky."

"Yeah yeah. Where's breakfast?"

She sat down and Jonah slid her her breakfast: a single pancake, four slices of bacon, and a bowl of strawberries with the tops cut off. He poured her a mug full of coffee, added cream and a just a bit of Splenda.

"Here baby." Jonah beamed.

"Thank you. Now go get dressed for your business trip, you don't want to be late!"

"Ah, it's fine, I don't have to be in Toronto until 5pm. I'd rather spend the morning with my family." Jonah answered, planting a kiss on Cole's head who murmured and snuggled into Jonah's chest.

"There might be traffic though, better safe than late. We need the money, babe."

"I guess you're right."

With Cole placed into his high chair, where his applesauce and pre-cut pancakes waited, Jonah climbed up the stairs, his family enjoying the meal behind him.

In his suit, Jonah knew if he dropped a pen it was game over. He fingered the suit's collar, with the vain hope of prying open a bigger airhole. No use. He unbuttoned the top button so he could get breath. He sighed and looked at the picture that dangled from the rearview mirror.

It depicted May holding Cole and himself holding a slightly too big Sara with Niagara Falls crashing behind them. His family's toothy smiles reflected the sunlight, and they all squinted so hard that their eyes were just slits. Sitting there in his cramped little Jetta with his knees nearly to his chest, he once again realized every sacrifice he ever made was worth it.

He reversed backwards from the driveway and was off to Toronto.

They had met in high school when Jonah was in the tenth grade and she in the ninth. Jonah was smitten, but she was way, WAY, above his caliber. For his entire high school career, his heart would erupt anytime he caught sight of the 4'11 girl in the hallways, her blonde hair swaying with her hips, hazardously avoiding getting stepped on by her enormous classmates. Jonah found himself taking the long way to class to pass by her. She always smelled of strawberry and coconut.

But Jonah had been a coward. It was not until his senior year when May was a junior when he had the nerve to ask her to the prom. He was pretty sure she only said yes to get into the senior prom, but it was a yes nonetheless.

The night was a blur, his suit collar choking him all night. They slow danced to Bon Jovi, and by the time the night was over they snuck back to May's house. She offered him a swig of her father's whiskey that she had stolen, and they lay on the grass in full suits and dresses, staring at the stars, giggling and drinking. And then something amazing happened. She lifted her head and placed it upon his chest. It had been the fourth happiest day of his life.

May passed out at two AM, right there in his arms.

That was when he knew he would marry her one day.

Jonah went to UofT for business, while May stayed behind to support her father who was passing away from kidney failure. In the days before the internet, they inevitably lost touch. Jonah never stopped thinking about her.

But then, one day, when Jonah was twenty-eight, he saw May for the first time in nearly a decade.

She was sprawled out on a park bench. Jonah would not have noticed her if not for the pitiful groan that erupted from her mouth as he walked. It was a wail that gripped his heart and stopped his feet in their tracks.

He looked at the sore sight upon the bench.

"May?" He asked.

A groan was his only answer from the supine woman.

Her once silken hair was matted, appearing like a bird's nest. She wore a torn jean jacket, far insufficient for the November air, sweatpants, socks, and a single tennis shoe.

He turned her head to the side and bile and vomit blasted onto Jonah's jacket.

He sat next to her and rolled her to her side. He rested her head on his jeans, pulled her hair behind her ears, and told her it was going to be ok.

The utilized needle rolling in the park path was not lost upon Jonah.

He looked in the rearview mirror towards the Cul-de-Sac and smiled at his beautiful, healthy family. He was so proud of May.

May waved goodbye and dragged herself back inside.

It would have been a great vacation if she wasn't stuck with Sarah and Cole the whole time. Thanks a lot, Jonah. Always skipping town to work, leaving her with the brats. Maybe she could find a babysitter without Jonah's indignant goddamn glances.

Sara hated when her father left. The cheery atmosphere immediately withered to tension. But tonight, she had a trick up her sleeve.

"Mom can I sleepover at Tanya's?"

May didn't even hesitate.

"Of course honey! In fact, why don't you pack a weekend bag and stay two nights?"

"If her mom says yes!" Sarah scampered back upstairs to pack her bag.

May smiled. Maybe she would be able to relax a bit this week, if she could just pawn off Sarah for the weekend. Plus, she knew exactly how to work Rochelle. She found her contact number and dialed.

"Hi Rochelle! So, Sarah was saying she could spend the night? I was really, really, really hoping you could take her for two. The baby is so overwhelming right now."

"Oh honey, of course, we don't need you all stressed all the time. Drop her off whenevs."

"Thank you love, kisses."

****

Tony smelled like weed and sweat, a smell that reminded

May of the nights of comfort the two had spent together.

She kissed his rough lips, silencing him, his bags dropping to the floor.

He pulled back, their eyes locking, but she held onto his neck tight. She never wanted to let go.

"Well, hi miss." He said in his low husky voice, electricity jolting up her spine.

His strong arms hoisted her, and she wrapped her legs tight around his waist. She looked down at his handsome face. Deep blue eyes stared into hers, his face chiseled and cut with a five o-clock shadow that May wanted to bury herself in. She tasted his minty breath once again and stole the piece of gum for herself.

"Hey now, be good miss."

"What if I'm not?"

He carried her upstairs, and she turned off the lights.

She lied in his muscular embrace, head empty.

"Babygirl, I brought you something."

"Oh? Haven't you don't enough?"

Tony rose from the bed, May's fingers gliding along his thigh.

From his black leather jacket, he produced the needle with the golden fluid.

Tony was gone. She was alone now, she realized. Her head pounded and she slunk to the kitchen for a cup of water. On the table, was a sticky note, and a needle.

"One more dose, until next time, miss."

She smiled, clutching the note to her chest.

This must be love, she thought. Not whatever reciprocity she felt towards Jonah, but real love. A man who went out of his way to give her gifts, and the best time. He never bothered her, never nagged. Why couldn't she just be with Tony?

A sigh escaped her dry lips as she hesitated over the last of her medicine in the syringe.

What was one more dose before she had to sleep next to the

withered sack that was Jonah again?

She injected it, pushing it down and down. May convinced herself to let her finger slip a little more, pushing more of the solution into her bloodstream.

*****

"How was your trip, dad?" Sarah asked, climbing out of the backseat.

"Oh not bad, Toronto traffic is always a pain is all. Thanks for asking sweetie."

"No problem. Can I have a popsicle?"

"Sure." Jonah said, a smile erupting on his face.

Jonah's briefcase swung to his hip, and he watched Sarah sail through the front door. He followed.

"Hello? I'm home!" Jonah called into the echoic house.

He climbed the stairs, placed his briefcase on his table, and hung up his jacket.

"Hello?" He called again.

"Dad?" Came Sarah's voice, fractured, from the kitchen.

There was his May, his beautiful beloved May, sprawled out on the kitchen floor with her head resting upon the refrigerator as if she were simply reading a book in bed. A syringe stabbed deep into her forearm, sticking out like an enemy's arrow that had found its mark. Her eyes were sucked into her skull with the pupils rolled downward to the floor. Vomit puddled around her like a sickly yellow aura.

"M...May?" Jonah asked, collapsing to his knees in front of her shaking her all too cold shoulders vigorously. "May!"

He gently brought her to the ground, cradling her head in his arms as he had when she drank too much on prom night, as he had when he found her all those years ago on the park bench. This time, he could already tell, was different.

Jonah looked at his daughter with hollow thoughts. Everything was so far away. He acted from a remote place, beyond the controls of his own mind. His voice seemed to come from somewhere else.

"Sarah, go call 911!"

She stood there, frozen, staring at her mother turned ghoul.

"NOW!" Jonah boomed, the first time he had ever raised his full voice to his daughter.

His highschool sweetheart, the love of his life, the mother of his children was ju-

Cole.

Jonah bolted up the stairs, crashing his hip into the banister with such force that it splintered. The baby's door flung open so hard the hinges rattled. Silence.

The crib was unmoving, but he could see the lumpy outline of his son through the crib posts. A cursed voice in his head told him not to look, he already knew what he would find. It was right.

Cole was facedown, still. He looked like a cast aside, sprawled out as if it were a child's baby doll, like one of the seven or so that Sarah had rotting in her closet. But this one was cold as ice.

Jonah fell to the floor, a blackness closed in on him from all sides and he wailed, the echoes haunting the halls of the house.

The ambulance was there in nearly record time, but it was already far too late for the infant who had not been tended to in over fifty one hours. Both May and Cole were declared dead on the scene, and carried away wrapped in sheets; Cole's white and May's stained with puke greens and yellows.

"Sir ?....Sir? is there somewhere that you and your dad would rather stay tonight?" A polite, professional paramedic asked the dazed father and daughter who sat on the porch, silent.

"Yes. At Tanya's." Sarah replied, as if it were just another regular sleepover with her bestfriend. Sometimes grief is slow in the mind of children, or simply tucks away under layers of mattresses of the mind as a morsel, a pea of trauma.

"That's a good idea, honey." Jonah said. They were the first words he had spoken in two hours.

"Would you like a ride?" The police officer who took their statements asked.

"No, sir. I will drive her."

The car ride was numb, and Jonah felt like he was operating a puppet man again.

Rochelle and Tanya were waiting outside for them when the car pulled into the driveway. Rochelle pulled Jonah into a hug that's warmth rivaled that of his grandmothers, he felt her tears on his cheek.

"Oh honey, oh sugar, I am so sorry darling. Is there anything you need, anything I can do?"

Tanya and Sarah were hugging in silence next to them.

"Thank you, Rochelle. Could you please watch Sarah for a few hours? I just need to be alone to… to process."

"Oh, of course baby, you go right ahead. Anything that you need I'm here for you baby." She slipped him a quick hug, then she turned her attention to Sarah, and Jonah was truly alone in the world.

He got back into the car and slammed the door leaving him in the hushed void of his own mind. He drove all the way home, empty, and pulled into the garage.

He walked through the empty house, echoing with the phantom of his child. She had fucking done this…. she had… everyone always told him he gave her too many chances. Her own mother had warned him away. But his goddamn fucking hero complex got him into trouble again, and again. Now she was dead. And lord knows, she fucking deserved it.

He looked at the hastily cleaned vomit upon the floor, highlighter yellow.

And he imagined his dead son, weighing less than 10 pounds, being jumbled around in a box to the crematorium. Only to be buried with his wife. His beautiful, lovely wife. His selfish, murderous, cunt of a spouse.

In his mind, Jonah saw her as she had been on Friday morning: oaken eyes gleaming in the sunlight, his son sitting on her hip, only now, her head was lolling to the side.

He crashed to the floor, on his hands and knees.

There, he saw the used condom, stuck to the floor.

His mind was emptied, cleared. Resolute.

The garage door slammed shut behind him. The engine of the car started. Jonah waited.

The sunlight gleamed through the window, catching the eternal chaos of dust particles in a creamy light. The doorbell rang. Rochelle answered the door to a pair of police officers. Sarah stared at her bowl of cereal; her mind was always foggy in the morning.

FRANKENSTEIN

Tony mopped the thick layer of ancient grease that glazed the kitchen floor making little difference to the yellow tiles that had been tread upon for decades. Eight hours in and a measly $120 in his pocket. That wouldn't even scratch the damn rent let alone the child support. He gazed at his sleeved arms, and he wished he could trade in the frivolous tattoos for cold, hard cash.

He heaved out a sigh into the indifferent air. Even then, he would be unable to crawl his way out of the dungeons of debt.

Best not to think about it. Get home, guzzle down a beer, and stare into the fuzzy abyss of satellite television. Eat Kraft Dinner, shower, sleep on his much too lumpy mattress, rinse and repeat until he died. Boy life just couldn't get any better.

"Tony, use figure eight form while mopping please, it's more efficient. Thank you." Gerald instructed, his long, hairless legs striding across Tony's clean floor.

Fuck you. Tony thought.

"Yes, sir." Tony said.

Gerald frowned. How could Tony mess up even the simplest of tasks? The shortstack meathead was all brawn no brain. He forgot to replace the napkins, refill the ketchup canisters, and once, he had even left his own wallet in the restaurant after closing. Gerald had had to return to unlock the door so Tony could retrieve it. His amateurism was exhausting, Gerald had enough kids to raise at home.

He settled in the back offices' armchair and began his daily paperwork. He had filled out the reports so many times that he could do so without paying much attention at all. Monotony was welcome as far as Gerald was concerned. It was soothing and relaxing, unlike the potential chaos that Tony could unleash at any moment. Pathetic, it was like he wasn't even a grown man, just an immature adolescent in the body of a pothead turned UFC fighter.

In front of Gerald three monitors displayed feeds of security cameras flickering their dull glow onto the desk. He stared at them, at the empty parking lot, the deserted dining area, and the kitchen where Tony, lo and behold, had failed to adopt the figure eight motion that Gerald had politely told him to.

Insolent kid.

A deep breath of stale office air filled his lungs. No need to get angry, stay in control.

"Tony!" He called, false enthusiasm coating his tone like syrup. "Figure eights!"

Tony clenched the handle. *Prick.*

Even with his back turned, Tony's gut pulled at the sound of the handgun cocking.

"Hands up." The voice was deep, calm. "Turn around."

The mop clattered to the floor and Tony spun around to face a gorilla of a man.

A tall man stood in the dining area wearing all black, down to the ski mask. He held a revolver pointed point blank at Tony's cranium. Tony imagined his skull popping open like a watermelon dropped on concrete.

In the office, Gerald's bug eyes stared at the monitor. His brain felt like a stuck record. He wanted to move, to help, but his slender glutes stayed glued to the office chair. He imagined himself reaching out, grappling for the landline and calling 911. But he stayed frozen, his synapses chilled to a stop.

"Hey, man, just take the money." Tony's hands shot in the air like he had seen a thousand time on *Cops.*

The man in black held the gun with pure control. Tony could feel the barrel pointing right between his eyes.

"Climb over the counter."

"Huh?" Tony asked.

"Do as I say, sir."

Tony vaulted over the low counter. His hip clashed against the cash register, a shock bolting into his core, the machine clattering to the ground sending bills fluttering into the air.

"Now bend over the table and pull down your pants."

"What?"

"You heard."

Tony grit his teeth and brought his chest down to the table. He undid his belt and slid his work pants down to his ankles.

"Underwear."

Tony slid the boxer briefs down his thighs, feeling the man's eyes molest his posterior.

"Where is your boss, sir?"

"In-in the back."

"Pull up your pants and go get him." The man instructed.

Tony felt a wave of relief as he tightened his belt back around his waist. He turned around, and made eye contact with sullen, sunken eyes the colour of gunmetal.

With the barrel of his snub nose, he waved Tony back toward the kitchen.

Tony considered beelining it through the back door of the kitchen, out to the parking lot, and vaulting the fence into the closed mall that lay on the other side. But it was futile. He knew his godforsaken stubby legs would never make it down the long hallway that led to the door in time. A bullet would catch him in the back without question. He already could feel it ripping through his lung, tearing the tissue straight from his chest. If only he had been born taller, faster.

Tony found Gerald rigid in his office chair, looking like a taxidermy doll, eyes locked upon the staticky security screens.

"Gerald, he wants you."

"Let's beat his ass." Gerald replied, hollowly. He wished he had the meat to back up his words. He had the height, but Gerald had always been a walking pole.

"What are you c...," Tony began replying.

The gun man was behind them now, cornering them into the small office. His shadow loomed over the two men.

"Let's go, out the back."

With obedience both men slunk in front of the gunman through the back door and into the damp night air.

Tony had been so close; his shift was almost done. He would have gotten home, cracked a cold one, and forgotten about Gerald and the damn child support wretch. Even this gunman didn't seem quite as bad as her. A cold one would do nicely about just now.

"Get in the Van, sirs." The gorilla gestured at an old van that Tony couldn't recognize. He had a dream of being a mechanic in his youth, but a kid at seventeen and a conniving baby mama can ruin those.

Gerald was still stiff, his movements mechanical, every muscle fiber straining under sheer panic.

Pussy. Tony thought.

Then he inhaled a mouth full of chloroform, and slumped face forward into the van.

The cell was dank. The smell of sweat, rusty iron, and mold wafted into his nostrils. Tony's eyes draped open. The blur of the drug slipping away like a forgotten dream.

Gerald was across from him, hung up on the wall with medieval style shackles that clanked as he struggled. Both their mouths were sealed with duct tape. Tony felt the bite of rusty irons around his own wrists and ankles.

Tony burst into a thrashing rage that lasted just seconds before he submitted to stillness and sunk his weight into the wall. A trickle of blood ran down his forearm.

Fuck. *He thought.*

If only he didn't fuck that conniving bitch he wouldn't have been working at the shit hole restaurant anyways.

"Fuck!" He tried to scream, but only a muffled yelp escaped the silver tape.

Salty tears dribbled onto the corners of his lips. Why was

he here? Who would want to kidnap some bums who work at a goddamn fast-food place? The question was fleeting; the man in black's "bend over" was pretty clear.

Fuck.

Gerald felt nothing but loathing. Tony had only been awake for under a minute, and he had already stopped resisting. His own wrists were bloody and raw, and he had been working on breaking his thumb. The anger bubbling in his veins at his useless employee seeped into his bound muscles and he raged with a refreshed fervor.

Tony watched Gerald yank and pull. Tony heard the popping of muscles as he strained and pulled against the restraints.

He's gonna break his goddamn wrist and still be trapped. Why struggle at all, dumbshit? We are restrained in medieval fucking iron shackles.

A thick door, submerged in shadows swung open with a deep clanging. The Gorilla stood there, still dressed in his robbery attire.

"Gentleman. I apologize for inconveniencing you in this way. Unfortunately, due to the laws of our time, we need to utilize…unwilling subjects for our procedures. I hope you can understand. Your sacrifices will not be in vain, I promise. Gerald, you will go first."

A familiar scent filled the air as the man in black strode to Gerald, ripped off the duct tape and forced a dampened blue and white cloth to his mouth. Gerald twisted and turned his head for fresh oxygen in vain, in retaliation the man gripped his thinning hair and slammed it into the cinderblock. Tony felt the reverberation from the blow in his own skull, wincing, and slumped downwards like a dog frightened of his owner.

"This can be easy." The man said, firmly placing the cloth over Gerald's nostrils. The exertion of a fruitless struggle brought nothing but the encroaching void to him sooner. The man in black slipped a key from his sock and unshackled Gerald. He let the thin man flop over his shoulders as if he was simply carrying a bag of potatoes.

The iron door slammed behind him, the deadbolt locking.

Tony waited. The minutes were agonizing and sluggish. Hours croaked by. A day, maybe. Tony wasn't sure. Time had no indication in the windowless hellroom.

He woke up to the rank breath of an unbrushed tongue. The figure, despite the sweltering heat, was dressed in black from head to toe. While equally big, this man wasn't the original gorilla.

"Morning. It's time, man." Without further warning, Tony inhaled a lungful of chloroform.

Tony knew not to resist as he faded into darkness and his captor unshackled the bolts. His sweat slathered back snapped off the wall as he fell to his knees.

The man hoisted him up with shocking strength.

Then he awoke.

An iron door across from him swung open, a blast of light rocking Tony's corneas. He squinted in the fluorescent gleam, the high squeal of the tube lights piercing his ears. Was he in a hospital? The interior was clean and smelled thick with medicine.

But he was bound.

The straps on the gurney were leather, thankfully.

Above him were doctors in blue surgical gowns and masks, and black sunglasses.

Then he realized that the squealing wasn't from the tube lights.

The screaming sawblade bit into his left hip like a soft tickle. He watched through sleepy eyes and thought that the thick layer of skin the surgeon sawed through looked rather like an orange peel. He felt the muscle and tendons of his legs snap like strings of taut licorice. She had to force it through the thick sinew that connected his femur to his hips, and Tony rocked back and forth with the motion.

The buttock was the easy part, the surgeon realized, soft as pulled pork thanks to the muscle relaxants and "feel good" drugs they administered.

She removed the detached limb and passed it to her partner.

He opened a large metal vault, cold steam erupting from within. He placed the limb in a pile amongst the others.

The smell of cooking meat wafted through the room. Tony stomach grumbled; it was like barbeque! Then he started to giggle, because he saw the smoke was coming from his own smoldering flesh as the surgeon cauterized his wound.

The doctor gazed at his alert eyes and motioned to another. Instantly, a purple fluid was injected into Tony's veins. The surge of warmth carried him into a deep, deep sleep.

Tony felt Miranda's delicate torso under his body weight. A hot sweat turning cold beneath the hotel's air conditioner at max setting. His heart pounded with exhilaration and relief. Was this love? She was perfect, and she loved him too. He could see it in her sparkling blue eyes, the way she looked at him. He pulled his neck up, but when he gazed down at her eyes only the huge, bug eyes of Gerald stared back at him.

Geralds mouth was caked with dry blood. He grunted and groaned, rocking back and forth, trying to shake Tony off of him.

He tried to get up. He didn't move an inch. The pushup simply wasn't working. He felt nothing below his palms.

He looked at his missing limbs. It made sense, that's why he couldn't get up. He swung his shoulder and managed to roll of Gerald with a soft thump onto the cold freezer floor.

Around him were sacks of what appeared to be potatoes all around him.

Then he screamed with the realization, but only a gurgling bloody moan breached the cold darkness. The melody of his cries reverberated, ten, fifteen others began to moan in unison, the room reverberating the haunting calls.

A singular lightbulb illuminated the cool room. Tony counted twelve other corpses, all men, all limbless and tongueless. Gerald lay down, staring at the ceiling, hope draining from his eyes in a stream of unending tears. Some men had managed to squirm themselves into a sitting position, propped up by the cold cinderblock wall. They all avoided eye contact with one another.

The smell was an unbearable mixture of sweat, dried blood, and urine.

Meals were tablets of protein and water. The man in black came and gave it to them all once daily and forced them into their tongueless mouths. The diet ensured there was little feces passed. Yet when men did go, they mostly just wallowed in their own filth, unmoving.

When the drugs ran out, Tony felt his limbs again, phantoms that squirmed under excruciating pains.

His mind went numb. He lost count of time. There was nothing. No movement, no fighting, no running. He pondered suicide, but how? Could he convey to Gerald or the other to bite his jugular? How would he convey such a thing? Gerald wasn't going to be of much help anyways. He lay as motionless as ever. Only the soft rising of his hairless chest told Tony there was still a flicker of life somewhere in there.

Somehow, when Tony thought of Gerald he was filled with joy. The sight of his next-to-motionless torso kept him conscious, on a string of hope for who knows what. Served him right to be like this.

The days ticked by excruciating boredom interrupted only by the occasional fleeting nightmare. Tony enjoyed them, it was better than his reality.

Tony was in a restless sleep when it happened. The man and black came and hoisted Tony onto his shoulder. Tony submitted to the motions and watched his companions fade into the darkness of the cold cellar.

He was thrown upon a table before seven to eight people dressed in business casual attire.

"EPPPPPPP!" Tony called, his best rendition of tongueless help.

The men and women snickered at him.

33

One of the people held up a sign with the number three.
Then four, a large man with greasy hair and pimples.
The sixth, an old woman with horrendous posture.
Then eight. He held up the sign.
Five.
Eight.
Six.
Eight.
Five.
Eight.
A gavel slammed next to Tony's skull.
Eight was a balding man, his hair combed over and brown. His smile rippled chills down Tony's spine. He brought a leather duffle bag onto the table, and pulled Tony into it. He zipped it shut, and the lights were out.

"That will be 65, 8."

"Heh, no problem. Business a pleasure as always. Hey could you de-eye for me?"

"For you, anything."

"I bet you are really confused." The man said in a scratchy voice.

Tony groaned, his only response.

"I guess one peak couldn't hurt, honey."

The man unzipped the duffle, the hospital light bursting in again.

He grabbed Tony gruffly by the hair, and yanked his neck up so he could see it.

A man, stumbling between two rehabilitation bars, as if learning how to walk.

His proportions were off...Tony recognized his own tattooed arms, and Gerald's long hairless legs.

The duffle bag shut, and Tony was carried away.

"Soak it up, sweetheart. It'll be the last thing you ever see."

CREEPY CRAWLIES

June 19, 2016

    I hate, hate, hate bugs. The way they squirm like they're aliens wriggling pulls my core into a tight ball. The fact that they can be anywhere, anytime, is the stuff of nightmares. How can people put up with them? One day, you could be sitting on your couch with your mom and the next day a black widow can have you writhing in agony. Mosquitoes swoop down from above, caring malaria and who knows what else. Leeches prevent me from swimming in any natural water source. Imagine if one were to writhe into the space between your toes, completely unknown until it has completely drained you of all your blood. Ticks? Have you heard of Lyme disease? I cannot deal with them. My therapist says it's good to write down my fears, so here I am journaling. I guess here it goes. I'm Lisa and this is my journey with entomophobia. They say just getting it out is the first step to healing.

June 21, 2016

    A centipede ran across my foot an hour ago. I am currently locked in my room, cross legged on my desk, with a towel stuffed underneath my door. I cried for half an hour, desperately scrubbing at my toes where it scuttled it's atrocious little feet. I stopped when it turned red and painful from the friction. I feel filthy, disgusting. What diseases could the abomination be carrying? Do you know they are venomous? I don't know what to do, it's still in my house somewhere. From now on I will be wearing my boots until I have proof it's dead. But I'm not crazy. I know that soon I'll have to face my fears and come out of my safe room. I can't stop thinking about the tiny abomination though. My therapist says I should write down my thoughts about bugs, and it will help me get over my fear. I think it's starting to help. Hopefully my cat, Gus, has managed to hunt it down. He's an exceptional bug hunter, I love him with all my heart for that. I'll be giving him some treats when I manage to work up the courage to get out of here.

June 22, 2016

I haven't seen the centipede. My good boy Gus must have taken care of him. I made him a can of tuna, and we cuddled the whole night away watching *Supernatural*. His resonating purrs against my chest are like a calming narcotic. I feel great today, I might even end up going out tomorrow.

June 23, 2016

I went to the farmers market today. It's usually something I avoid, thinking about all the creepy crawlies that have been in and out of the untreated produce and that makes me want to vomit. Or worse, I ponder the flies buzzing around the fruit. But I did it! I went out! Maybe it really is the journaling that has been calming me down. I should bake my therapist a pie. Anyways, I'm going to make a fresh salad! Things are looking up, and I'm not looking down. (Haha, get it?)

June 24, 2016

Today is the worst fucking day of my life. While I was making breakfast this morning, a PREGNANT spider zipped across the floor. Before I had a chance to do anything, I watched Gus pounce on it from the kitchen table and gobble it up like it was a treat. I was about to thank him, but then something occurred to me…what if the spider has babies inside of him? They will need nutrients when they hatch, and they would eat Gus inside out. Anytime an animal dies in the woods, it gets festered by bugs who slowly gnaw at the insides until there is nothing less but withered mummy of the inedible bits. The idea of Gus being food for baby spiders sent the feeling of the bugs crawling up my arms and into my mouth into my brain. I instantly scooped him up, threw him in the back seat of my car, and sped to the clinic. He sat there innocently, staring at me in the rearview mirror with a confused look on his face, a sparkle in his emerald eyes. My poor boy is dying, and it was all my fault.

I took him to the vet but the veterinarian is a fucking idiot! I told him what happened, and he insisted there is nothing to worry about, but I watched Gus eat a gut full of spider babies! He is going to die, and the vet told me it's all a ok.

My poor boy, I don't know what to do. I can't even bring myself to cuddle him, what if the creatures burst from his eyes sockets in a swarm? So, I locked him in the bathroom with food and water so I can think this out.

June 25, 2016

I woke up this morning, praying that last night was a nightmare. But no, the scratching and meowing of the bathroom door snapped me back to my infested reality. He was suffering in there. I needed to do something. I called the vet pleading for him to come, reiterating that it was a poisonous, pregnant spider he had consumed. The doctor still asserted that it was fine. I will have to research some medicine on my own.

June 25, 2016

Online, it says a consumed spider can kill a cat if it was bitten on the throat, mouth, or stomach lining. However, there is nothing about pregnant spiders. This could be the first documented case of a cat eating one. They are inside him now, eating my poor Gus from the inside out. I... I don't know what to do. I have to get the bugs out of him, I can't let him die. I just have to think of a way to get them out of him.

June 26, 2016

I cut a quarter sized incision into Gus's belly with a kitchen knife. He screamed and cried in my arms, but I held him tight around the neck as his blood began to seep into his golden ginger fur. Even in all his pain, he didn't scratch or bite me. That's because he knew I was helping him. He squirmed, but I held him down firmly with my left hand. Inside of his tissue, I saw them. The little black eggs of spiders, embedded in his pink flesh. Unmistakably spider eggs, what else would be in the muscle and fat tissue of a cat? My boy is dying, and all I need to do is pluck out the eggs to save him. There's a problem though, I can't hold him down and pluck out the eggs with just two hands. I need some supplies to knock him out. Luckily, having a past has its rewards.

June 26, 2016

Joel didn't forget to remind me that I look like shit. Funny coming from a ketamine dealer who looks like he hasn't slept in years. Either way, got the K and told him to piss off. I got a large thin knife, tweezers, and a large roll of bandages to make sure he was ok after my improvised surgery. I don't want to hurt my baby, but it's for his own good. The spiders WILL kill him.

June 26

The K worked wonders on Gus. He lay still and his breathing was faint, like that of a sleeping baby. Slicing deep into his soft belly flesh felt freeing. Like that feeling when you pop a nasty pimple and instantly feel relief. A good pain. I sliced a very thin incision from his neck down to just above his genitals. Then, I dug through the sinew and fat, searching for the lumps that I had found yesterday with the tip of my fingers. I dug them out and threw them down the sink. There was lots of blood. I think it hurt me more than him, but now that his stomach flesh is clear I'm certain he will be fine. Unless…the eggs have spread to the rest of him already.

I need to get the rest of his muscles. Tomorrow, I'll do his limbs, then back, then head. That way he can have a rest. At least he will be escaping with his life.

June 27

When I woke up this morning, Gus was hiding behind the recycle bins in the garage. He was still dozy, so I was able to catch him. I was hurt, my poor boy hissed at me. I mean I get it, I'm not crazy, he's suffering a lot of pain. But still, after everything I did to help him? He just can't understand it's for his own good. I jolted the needle into his neck and administered another dose of K. His stomach bandages are bloodied, but not bled through.

I worked on his legs. By making long, thin incisions down each limb, I could just squish the tweezers around, in and beneath his bones. Tough work, and it took several hours, but when I was done I had pulled out hundreds of eggs. I threw each one into a fire that blazed outside in the grey atmosphere. No chances.

Tomorrow, I'll get his back and face.

June 28

I'm broken. I found Gus dead behind the recycling bins this morning. The spider's venom must have infused into his bloodstream before I could remove all the eggs. My poor boy, he's dead. All because of bugs. It's as if everyone's in on it to make me feel crazy! The bugs KILLED GUS. How can everyone just act like they're ok with all the bugs! I tried to tell the doctors, I tried!

My mind is swarmed now with images of his infected flesh, slowly rotting away as the spider eggs sucked nutrients from the host.

But it just hit me... was it not possible that I had consumed an egg myself? Through a pore on my skin, or maybe I inhaled it. I shouldn't have treated Gus. I should have shot him humanely or bag him in a garbage bag and move him three cities over. Now... now he's infected me with the eggs.

I must go to the hospital. With the evidence, surely, they'll treat me, right?

June 29

Theirs bugs in me theirs bugs in me theirs bugs in me and

the hospital won't let me get them out! They think I'm crazy, but I saw the bugs, the spiders, the eggs. They want me to go to therapy. Therapy! My cat is literally dead because of the bugs that they wouldn't help me with, and now they want me to go to therapy! Do they not understand that the bug eggs are inside of me right now? I am going to die, and it is due to the public and private health care system. Unless I take matters into my own hands. For Gus, I have to keep on trying. Keep on living.

June 30.

I tried using a knife to cut along my shin bone the same way I had for Gus. I couldn't take the pain. But the knowledge that they're in me is so much worse. I needed something less intrusive than the knife. Then my mind drifted over to the potato peeler and the idea became clear. If I can simply skin my...skin...with something like a potato peeler I could pick out the eggs. I don't have to carve myself with a knife like some kind of psychopath. I can feel the spiders under my skin, crawling around like children under their mamas blanket. I can't describe my agony; I have to do this. I'm going to start now.

June 30

The pain was debilitating but I pushed through. My leg skin sits in a folded file upon a garbage bag. I dug out hundreds of tiny eggs, burning them by throwing them into the hearth flames. My legs look like two slabs of raw beef, but clean beef. I downed close to 12 Advil's, finished the ketamine, and put on bandaged. But I still feel the spiders. I HEAR them starting to hatch, crawl around. My arms are nearly raw from my scratches already. I will now begin cleansing my arms. I HAVE TO GET THE BUGS

All my legs and arms are naked to the world, there might be bugs

And I'll put my legs in the fire, to burn out the eggs., the healing power of the flames burn the spider bugs eggs. I am taking a break now to journal. My therapist says it will help me get rid of bugphobia.

Jules placed down the diary and looked at the flayed corpse upon the bed. The burns puffed and bloated her body to a charred blister. Blood and pus seeped into the sheets. Grotesquely, the image of lasagna popped into his mind: the blood and guts as the sauce, the skin the noodles. He held the butt of his fist of his mouth, determined not to vomit in the crime scene.

He sprinted out of the room and into the washroom, where he was greeted by the corpse of Gus, the interior of the bathtub caked in dry brown stains.

Jules's vomit sprayed in the toilet, and he stumbled to the kitchen to take a seat.

A small black spider crawled across his hand.

DEMONS

I've been possessed by demons my entire life. The thing is, those sonsofbitches are sneaky. Pure evil, straight from the depths of hell. They can ruin your life without you even knowing it.

I guess I was eight when I first felt the demons in me. Me and Tommy were at the playground, and I was pushing him on the swing. One of those nostalgic nights where the crickets are chirping, and the setting sun is warping the sky into a sherbet of colours. That was my last happy thought, I reckon.

When he swung back, I grabbed his ass with my hands and pushed. It was an accident, I think, but I still did it. Something inside me *made me* do it. I felt his soft cheeks beneath my palms, the soft but slender buttocks squishing in between my fingers. We kept playing like normal, but right then I felt something wrong in my gut. We laughed and played and walked home like everything was ok. The only difference was this time I had a stomachache.

That night I was watching tv with my parents and Tommy was sitting in my lap like usual. And that's when I got the first boner I can ever remember. It had to be a real one, not something I did on accident because I didn't even know what a boner was at the time. Hard, erect and raging, rising beneath my brother's butt. The demon inside me made me do it, and I just kept watching the show like a fuckin creep with my little brother on top of my dick. God, it makes me sick to think about it.

My stomach groaned with unknown guilt, ashamed of the change in my body. The next day I asked my mom what it meant when your penis got really hard. She told me, fairly enough, to ask my pops about that one. I remember running down the hallway, the panic of guilt having spread to my fingers now. Why wouldn't my mom tell me?

I stumbled down the stairs and blurted out my question. My father laughed boomingly, and pulled me into an embrace. He told me that that is what happens when you really like something a lot. He was a few beers in, so he asked me who had given me my first stiffy. I laughed, and thinking he was proud of me, told him about Tommy sitting on my lap when we were watching the movie.

The atmosphere dropped like a damned anvil. Imagine your kid telling you they got a raging hard on from their kid brother? What would you even tell that kid?

He laughed. Fucking laughed.

"What are ya, some kind of pedophile?"

"What is a pedophile?" I asked.

Instead, he just laughed and walked away.

The next day at school, I asked a bunch of older kids I was playing soccer with what a pedophile was. One kid told me his uncle was a pedophile, and that he went to jail for doing evil things to his cousin with his penis. That's when I knew that I had to do everything in my power to contain the evil for the rest of my life. Or else I could hurt someone. In fact, I already had.

Since that day, I avoided Tommy every time I saw him, just in case I accidently touched him or, God forbid, got another boner because of him. The thought ate my up. I had endangered my own kid brother.

We grew distant fast. His questioning eyes scanned me, looking for the reason I was ignoring him. Unfortunately, I couldn't completely phase him out. Mom made me walk him to school, and what's worse is she made me hold his hand. The grossest part was I enjoyed the contact with him. I hid behind the excuse my mom was making me, but it was just because I am a creep.

What would God think of me? Father Jim says he forgives everything but there's no way he would forgive this. I was, and am, a pedophile. I'm a sinner destined for hell.

One day, about a month into my discovery I was in my

bedroom reading a book, just trying to blot out the thoughts that that screamed my sins against on repeat. When Tommy let himself into my room. I bolted up in my bed, shoving the covers over my crotch in case I got another hard-on.

"What!" I yelled.

His eyes were blue pits. A gaping sinkhole opened in my chest.

"How come you don't hang out with me anymore."

We stared each other down, I was filled with rage, anger, guilt and disappointment. So many emotions I couldn't even process.

"Because you're an annoying little shit! Get out of my room!" And I chucked my novel at him.

I passed my days in the library, reading books and avoiding my house. When I read, there were pockets of blissful moments in which I forgot about my sins against my little brother. When I wasn't reading, all I could think about was Tommy, and how evil I was.

Years passed, and I somehow buried the guilt deeper and deeper. The demon was still there, clawing its way to the surface in the form of evil thoughts. You are evil. You will hurt someone again, soon. You are a pedophile. But in between these moments, I was able to function. Get passing grades in school. Even start to hang around with Tommy again. Yet, there was always the rift of guilt and potential harm between us.

I realized why he was being so distant. I knew why he had begun avoiding me. It was because he knew what I was. He was the only one who truly knew who I was. The evil, rapist, older brother. I could still feel his buttocks against my lap, and his hips upon my hands. Even my dreams weren't safe from all the guilt, I had nightmares of me having full blown sex with my little brother. What kind of sicko dreams about having sex with their own little brother?

So I started to wash myself. My hands, every time I could *feel* his young body beneath my hands. By the time I was 12, my hands were raw and red. Cuts and sores appeared deep in my flesh, which I seared again and again under the soap and water. The doc diagnosed me with eczema, a skin condition I guess, but it was really from the soap eating away at the oils on skin before they healed.

My crotch looked the same, raw from the attempted washing away from my sins, from my genitals down to just above the knees. Wearing underwear chaffed away and me in itchy pain so I began to go commando.

The washing continued until I was 14 and found a better distraction than the local library. Books were nothing compared to the bliss that was alcohol. When I was 16, my father gave me my first shot of whiskey at the family Christmas party. I felt the warm firewater burn down my throat, and for the first time in over half a decade, I felt like talking.

In fact, that was the first night me and Tommy spoke, really talked, since I found out I was a pedophile. I told him I always loved him no matter what, and I was sorry we had drifted so far apart. We hugged deeply.

When I woke up the next morning, mind wild with anxiety, I realized I had used alcohol as an excuse to touch Tommy again. I was, am, a monster using booze to work up the courage to do what I knew was evil. To do what the demons made me do.

I needed to go away for school, somewhere I couldn't hurt my little brother.

I went to school for engineering. The weight of my studies was colossal on my shoulders but I was able to rely on my good ol' pal whiskey for getting me through the damn degree. Otherwise, the thoughts would have made me off myself, I reckon.

Booze, in all their glory, also led to the night that ruined my life for good.

I was a junior when it happened. Me and my buddy John were at a house party, slamming back shots with some fine women. I managed to score one's number, she was a fine piece too. Long legs and a butt so good it would make any man crumble. And somehow, my drunken ass had convinced her that she wanted me.

Me and John took a celebratory shot.

Then, I woke up in my dorm bed sopping with cold sweat and my mouth dry as a desert. My heart ran like a racehorse. I tossed my head over the side and yakked my damn brains out. When I looked down, I was still in my polo and jeans, caked with the same green barf that was encrusted into the carpeted floor.

I stumbled to the kitchen and poured myself a cup of water, my head feeling like I was 20 feet under in the community pool. I chugged it down. Then I remembered the dime pieces from last night. Did I really blow it because of too much booze?

Answer: Yes.

I called John. He filled me on the rest of the night.

My dumbass had thrown up on one of the girls, so I never got to take her home. Apparently I was mad pissed off at myself so John and I went to the park to roll up. We sparked, and then he said I walked home piss drunk with the bluest balls ever.

But the thing was, I didn't feel like it. I felt like I had the best goddamn sex in my life.

"You hear the news?" John asked after he was done relaying my drunken expedition. "You didn't see anything that night, did you? It was so close to us."

"Honestly, I was drunker than a wasp in an orchard. I can't even remember going to the park. What happened?" I asked.

A boy had gone missing from the very park where we lit up the night before. Richy Nguyen, 8 years old, had last been seen by their friends at the very damn park me and John were at.

It was me.

It had to be me.

I had buried it beneath the parties and scholarly distractions, but deep, deep down, I knew. I was still the same pervert rapist that molested my own little brother all those years ago.

Who's to say that I hadn't done the same damn thing, or something far, far worse, to that little kid? My stomach felt like it sucked in my other organs, my heart pounded as if it were angry at me. I couldn't live that way.

So I went somewhere I never thought I'd go again, the

Church. Good old Father Jim was still the pastor. If only I could be him, in all his perfection. But I was, am, tainted. I felt like I would be smited just for walking into the church, but the oak doors swung in with a foreboding woosh.

Inside, the interior was just as I remembered it. Nothing had changed other than my perception. The pews were empty, and my eyes were drawn to where my family I sat down on our asses. Tommy's ass. Even in God's house, I could do nothing but think of sinning. Nothing had changed, other than my perception.

The Church felt empty and hollow without people in it. Or maybe it was because God had left knowing I was there. Yet still, there remained Father Jim sitting with his now balding head in the first pew with his back turned.

"Father Jim?" I asked into the echoic church.

"Well, ain't that old young Carl Jones? The devil must be playin' tricks on me." He croaked.

"It is." Normally, I would make pleasentries but my head swarmed with the wasps of self-hatred, and I ached for relief. "Father, I would like to make a confession."

"Why, of course my son." The welcoming smile vanished from his face as if he sensed the dire tone in my words.

The church still had those old confession boxes where you can hear but not see the priest. It almost made it easier for me to spit out the bile that was the truth.

"How many years has it been since your last confession?

I felt the weight of my sins upon my shoulders. "Almost a decade."

Then the words started to stream out, the wasps in my skull buzzing and stinging with ferocity.

"I have done lots of sins father. Ever since I was a little boy. I have to... have to tell someone."

"Of course my son."

"This is confidential right?

"Of course my son."

"I am gay. I always look and men and feel strange feelings of guilt. I know God tells me it's wrong. I feel that it's wrong, but I just can't stop myself from glancing."

"Oh....Well, son, many very godly men are gay. You are not a sinner for something that you cannot control."

I should have felt relief. But that was just the warm up.

"I... I'm a pedophile. I like people that are a lot younger than me."

"Oh...how long have you known this son?"

"Since I was eight, I guess." I knew.

"Well, there is nothing wrong with being attracted to children when you are a child yourself. Do you still have these feelings?" He asked me.

"I always think about... I always think about Tommy when he was younger. I was attracted to him, and I... I did some really bad things to him."

"What did you do to him?" Father Jim asked quickly.

"I touched him, molested him."

Father Jim was silent, as if he was weighing the severity of my sins against the strength of Gods forgiveness.

"When was the last time you did something like this."

And there it was. The bowling ball in my chest that I just couldn't carry anymore. It was time to cough it up. The wasps swarmed and howled in excitement that could be either anger or glee.

"I... I think I killed and raped Richy Nguyen."

Seconds trickled away like sand in an hourglass. The silence tore at my ear drums.

"You must turn yourself in, or I will."

You'd think I would feel betrayed. Only minutes ago, he had promised me his confidentiality. Maybe I should have tore through the fragile wooden screen at his throat, leave him a bloody corpse on the floor of his very own church. But no, that's not how I felt at all. A great swell of relief rushed through me; it was no longer my burden alone to bear. I could stop hiding like the slimy criminal I was, and people would know the true me.

"Yes Father."

"God will forgive you my son. May the justice system as

well."

I phoned the police on the church's landline.

"911 what is your emergency?"

"Hi, my name is Carl Jones, and I would like to confess to a crime."

"Well son, this isn't really the place…"

"I raped and killed Richy Nguyen.

The woman was silent.

"Police are on the way to your location now."

The cops broke my jaw, two ribs, and my right femur during the interrogation. I wish I could have done it to myself. I relished under their blows, crying tears not of sadness but joy for finally feeling the punishment for all my past sins.

I told them everything I could remember, the day it started beneath my palms at the park, and how I had preyed first upon my little brother Tommy. The cop asked if I had gotten sick of Tommy and wanted to move onto something younger. I said yes.

They wanted to know where I had hidden the body, but lord knows that I had no idea. The wasps and fumes of stagnant alcohol clouded the truth even from me.

The court date arrived. I was unshaven and unkempt, as disgusted with myself on the outside as I was with myself on the inside. At least I had the catharsis of knowing the truth was out, I was hiding no longer.

My court-appointed lawyer seemed to have as little interest in keeping me out of jail as I did. He glared laser beams at me through, beady, judging eyes. They meant nothing to me. His opinion could not be worse than the one I held of myself. I am a slimy, preying parasite.

Tommy showed up to my court date. Until then, it felt like a dream but the face of my brother brought me crashing back into the defendants chair. I clutched the desk and began to sweat.

He had shown up as a character witness. For whatever reason, he vehemently denied every claim I had made against myself that involved him in any way. He said I was always a strange older brother and distant, but never ever harmful.

But why would he lie? Why was he here? We hadn't spoken in over five years.

It didn't matter anyways. The judge threw the book at me, my confession shielding me only from life in prison. Sixty years. I felt a relief wash over me, finally true attonment could be served. I just hoped that Father Jim, Tommy, and God could forgive me when it was all through.

Prison wasn't the worst thing once I got used to the abuse of the other inmates. It started when they cornered me in the bathroom. I'm sure I don't have to tell you what happens to kid diddler prisoners. But they took me, and I knew I deserved it.

When they were done with me, I looked like a swollen monster. I bled, the lacerations tearing every time I took a step. I spent the following week curled up on my cot, tears streaming from my eyes. But not for me, for the ones that I had harmed. It lasted months, but eventually, those who used me got bored and moved on. Just as done to Tommy, cast aside like rotting meat.

All my life, I had avoided looking at myself in the mirror as all I could ever see staring back were the demons. But in the cells, it's hard to avoid glancing at that tiny, plastic framed mirror. When I did, I saw a hollow husk, as withered on the outside as within. I didn't see the demons behind my eyes; I had become the demon.

They found Richy Nguyens corpse last week. It was found buried in the church graveyard when a particularly bad rainstorm removed the layer of topsoil, and his little decomposing hand reached out of the muck as if someone could pull him back out alive and well.

Yesterday, they cleared me for release. The DNA testing showed that I didn't do it.

Printed in Great Britain
by Amazon